Hello, Big Jay!

Aimee Aryal

Illustrated by Anuj Shrestha

www.mascotbooks.com

It was a beautiful day at
the University of Kansas.

Big Jay was on his way
to Allen Fieldhouse
to watch a basketball game.

He walked past the Kansas Union.

Some students standing nearby said,
"Hello, Big Jay!"

Big Jay passed by the Campanile where
he met some alumni.

The alumni remembered Big Jay
from their days at KU.
They said, "Hello, again, Big Jay!"

Big Jay walked to Strong Hall.

A professor walking by waved,
"Hello, Big Jay!"

Big Jay stopped at the Watson Library.

A librarian who works inside
said, "Hello, Big Jay!"

Big Jay walked to the statue of Phog Allen outside Allen Fieldhouse.

He ran into some Kansas fans there.
They yelled, "Hello, Big Jay!"

Finally, Big Jay arrived on
the basketball court.

As he ran onto the court, the crowd chanted, "Rock Chalk, Jayhawk, KU!"

Big Jay watched the game from the sidelines and cheered for the team.

The Jayhawks scored a basket!
The players shouted,
"Slam dunk, Big Jay!"

At halftime the KU Band performed
for the audience.

Big Jay and the crowd sang,
"I'm a Jayhawk."

The Kansas Jayhawks won
the basketball game!

Big Jay gave the basketball coach
a high five. The coach said,
"Great game, Big Jay!"

After the basketball game, Big Jay
walked down the Hill. It had been
a long day at the University of Kansas.

He walked home and climbed into bed.

"Good night, Big Jay!"

For Anna and Maya,
and all of Big Jay's little fans. ~ AA

For my buddy, Himal. ~ AS

For more information about our products,
please visit us online at www.mascotbooks.com.

For more information, please contact Mascot Books,
P.O. Box 220157, Chantilly, VA 20153-0157

ISBN: 1-932888-41-1

Printed in the United States.

www.mascotbooks.com